How The Tortoise Broke His Back

For Vanessa
Anything & everything is possible

ISBN 0 9546116 0 8

Printed in Great Britain

First published in 2003 by

AMLAP PUBLISHING

PO Box 6144, Basildon,
Essex SS14 0WX

How The Tortoise Broke His Back

Adapted from African Folk Tales

Paula B Sofowora

Illustrated by
Lisa Parsons

MANY years ago, animals walked the earth on two legs just like man. They talked, ate, and did just about everything, like we do today.

'Ijapa' the tortoise was known to be one of the wiliest of all the animals because of his wit and cunning. This is the story of how he broke his back, and why to this very day you can still see the pattern left on his shell.

In those days, all the animals were friends and did things together. All the birds were preparing for their annual conference in the sky. Traditionally, a lavish feast followed this, and everybody who was anybody wanted to be invited to it.

Ijapa received an invitation to be the honorary chairman. Oriole, one of the elders, chose him because of his reputation for being witty and wise.

Invitation

We have great pleasure in inviting you to be the Honorary Chairman at the ANNUAL CONFERENCE

Oriole

BIRDS of all different shapes and sizes and motley colours, donated a few feathers, so that Ijapa could have his very own pair of wings. For the special day, the birds wanted their honorary guest to look like them, and fly like them.

EVERYTHING went according to plan. The wings were beautiful. Ijapa could not stop looking in the mirror and preening himself. Yanibo, his wife, and all the other animals agreed that he looked very grand indeed. They secretly wished that they had received an invitation too.

On the day of the conference, all the animals were dazzled by the brilliant, vibrant colour in the sky. There was the sound of sweet melody as the birds called to each other on their way.

IJAPA had his very own escort to ensure that there was no mishap.

IJAPA made a speech with his usual pomp and show. Every one present listened eagerly to what he had to say. Some whispered to one another about how wise Ijapa was, and how fortunate they were that he had agreed to be their chairman.

In the course of his address, Ijapa told all the delegates to choose a nickname. It sounded like a good idea at the time, and every one agreed. Ijapa chose the name, 'For Everyone'.

The conference was progressing well. Sweet aromas were beginning to waft into the conference hall.

Ijapa and all the other delegates were starting to get hungry. They fidgeted as the stewards brought in steamy dishes of assorted food.

Each time the stewards addressed the chairman, they said, 'This is For Everyone'. Parrot and Swallow were about to help themselves, when Ijapa reminded them that the dish was for him, 'For Everyone'.

TO the stunned amazement of all the delegates, Ijapa proceeded to 'demolish the dish.' The stewards continued to come out with more delicious food, and each time addressed the chairman, 'This is For Everyone.' Ijapa remembered his manners and repeatedly said, 'Thank you', while Oriole and the hungry birds angrily looked on.

It was well known that Ijapa was greedy. But nobody realized that by the time he had had his fill, there would hardly be anything left. In disgust, the birds began to leave one by one. As they did, they removed the feathers that they had given him. Ijapa was stranded.

Suddenly, he had a brilliant idea. A Cuckoo was perched on a tree near by. 'Cuckoo', he said, 'will you take a message to Yanibo? Tell her to bring out all the mattresses, cushions, and pillows, so that I do not hurt myself when I jump down.'

CUCKOO promised to deliver the message. He had heard about what happened at the conference, and felt someone needed to teach Ijapa a lesson. 'Yanibo,' said Cuckoo, 'Ijapa said that you should bring out everything sharp and dangerous in the house and spread them on the ground.'

Yanibo was puzzled by this message, but she knew better than to question the wisdom of her husband. She obeyed without question, and brought out all the knives, cutlasses, barbed wire, broken glass, and pots that she could find. She arranged them in front of the compound just as Cuckoo had asked her to.

CUCKOO flew back and told Ijapa that he had delivered the message to Yanibo, and it was safe for him to jump down.

Well, the birds had the last laugh. They all gathered round to see the spectacle that followed.

Ijapa jumped and landed on all the sharp and dangerous objects. He broke his shell in lots of little pieces. Yanibo had to stick them all back together again. He still has the same pattern on his back. Have you noticed it? Next time you see a tortoise, have a closer look.

What is the moral of this story?

The answer is on the next page.

Don't be too smart.

Remember, someone else may have the last laugh!

What do you remember?

1. Who is Yanibo?
2. What nickname did Ijapa choose for himself?

Can you spell these words?

Tortoise   Conference   Honorary

Do you know the meaning of these words?
(Use your dictionary to help you).

Wily   Lavish   Fidget   Spectacle   Motley

Do you know what the following expressions mean?

'pomp and show'   and   'demolish the dish'

Name 3 types of bird that are mentioned in the story.

Other titles in this series:

Why the Tortoise is Bald

For details of other titles available
from Amlap Publishing, please write to:
Amlap Publishing, PO Box 6144, Basildon, Essex, SS14 0WX